CUENTO
DE LUZ

DOROTHY: A Different Kind of Friend

Text © Roberto Aliaga
Illustrations © Mar Blanco
This edition © 2013 Cuento de Luz SL
Calle Claveles 10 | Urb Monteclaro | Pozuelo de Alarcón | 28223 | Madrid | Spain | www.cuentodeluz.com
Original title in Spanish: DOROTHY, una amiga diferente
English translation by Jon Brokenbrow

ISBN: 978-84-15619-81-9

Printed by Shanghai Chenxi Printing Co., Ltd. January 2013, print number 1335-03

FSC
www.fsc.org
MIX
Paper from
responsible sources
FSC® C007923

DOROTHY

A Different Kind of Friend

Roberto Aliaga   Mar Blanco

Dorothy is my best friend.
We don't look much like each other at all
because she's got more hair than me.
And she's **much bigger** than me.
And she doesn't talk as much as I do.

But we have a great time
when we're together.

Nearly every morning
we meet up to go swimming in the river.
Dorothy floats on her back
and we drift downstream with the current for hours.

She is the island and I am the shipwrecked sailor.
But I'm not lonely.

At lunchtime, Dorothy takes me back to her house, and without anyone knowing, hides me under the table.

I get enough to eat
just from the crumbs
that fall from the table.

**Since we've been friends,
I've never been hungry.**

And in the afternoon, once we've had a nap,
we usually go out for a stroll.
I sit on her shoulders and sing into her ears,
or I tell her stories that she's never heard.

I know Dorothy loves them,
even though she pretends she can't hear me.

She's my best friend.
Nobody knows her as well as I do.
When Dorothy's happy,
the birds settle down to sleep on her head.
And when she's angry, the earth trembles in fear.

But we can't always be together.

If I want to go swimming in the river with
the others, Dorothy can't come with me.
They don't like my friend.

When they see me coming,
they stop looking in their mirrors
and start **to yell**.

I tell them that Dorothy isn't a thing; she's my friend. But they don't care, and they kick up the same fuss as every other day:

Of course, so I don't get angry with them
and to stop them from saying horrid things
about my friend, I have to tell them:

"Don't worry, I came on my own.
Dorothy doesn't know where I am."

They look around in a funny kind of way,
as if they think I'm tricking them.

But after a while they go back to where they were sitting
and carry on with what they were doing.

They've already forgotten about Dorothy.
They don't have very good memories
because their heads are too full of

princess stuff.

I sit down by the pool and splash my feet in the water.
Normally, I don't do anything much. Well, I do.
I usually think about Dorothy ...

... until the trees around us start
to shake, a shadow covers the sun,

and Dorothy suddenly appears!

She doesn't do it on purpose,
but she flops into the pool like a
boulder and covers everyone in mud.

argh!!! *

The others get angry.
Most of them scream; some pretend to faint.

I grab Dorothy's hand and we run off together, saying we're sorry:

**"Don't worry,
it won't happen again!"**

Once we're far away, Dorothy looks into my eyes to see if I'm angry.
I always say the same thing:

"How could I be angry with you?
It was a lovely dive!"